# HUAN CHING AND THE GOLDEN FISH

Story by Michael Reeser

Illustrations by Dick Sakahara

Raintree Publishers
Milwaukee

In memory of my grandmother, Lenora Pool,
who was very dear to my heart.

—M.R.

For Arleen, with love.

—D.S.

1 2 3 4 5 6 7 8 9     92 91 90 89 88

Library of Congress Number: 88-18579


**Library of Congress Cataloging-in-Publication Data**

Reeser, Michael.
  Huan Ching and the golden fish.

  Summary:  A grandfather competes against his grandson in a
kite flying contest on Chung Yang Chieh, the Chinese kite flying
holiday.
  [1.  Kites—Fiction.   2.  Grandfathers—Fiction.
3.   Children's writings]   I.  Sakahara, Dick, ill.   II.  Title.
PZ7.R2553Hu    1988        [Fic]         88-18579
ISBN 0-8172-2751-2

My name is Huan Ching. I am one of the grandsons of the great Huan Ching of China. Today is the day of Chung Yang Chieh or the kite flying holiday. We are going up to the mountain to fly our kites. All the boys and men in the whole land will be there. The women and girls will bring a great feast.

The boys and men will compete against each other to see who has the best kite. Then we will have wars with our kites. While the kites are flying, we will try to cut each other's strings with our own strings. I hope I win this year.

7

This will be the first time that I have ever gone to the Chung Yang Chieh. I have spent months working on my kite. It is a goldfish, and the scales have an outline of light blue. Inside the scales, there is gold glitter. My kite is about three feet high and five feet long.

The reason I chose a fish is that in China we believe that a fish kite brings health, wealth, and fortune to whoever owns it. But there will be many kinds of kites there, not just fish kites. There will be bat kites because bats are supposed to live many years. There will also be butterfly kites because a butterfly means pleasure and a happy marriage.

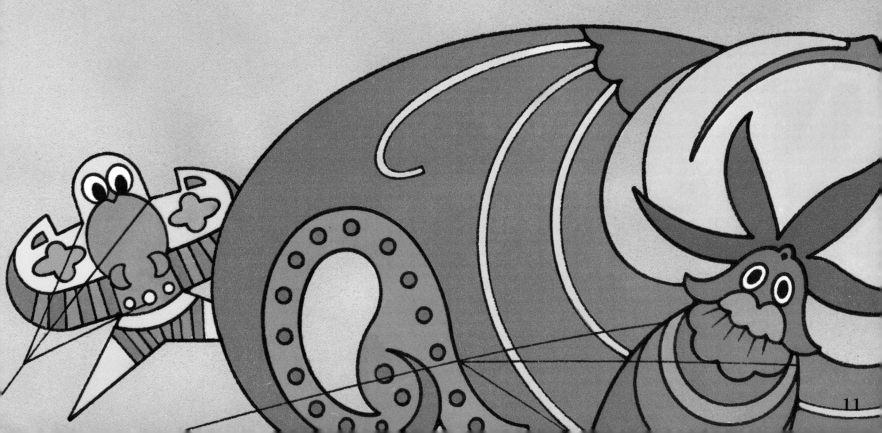

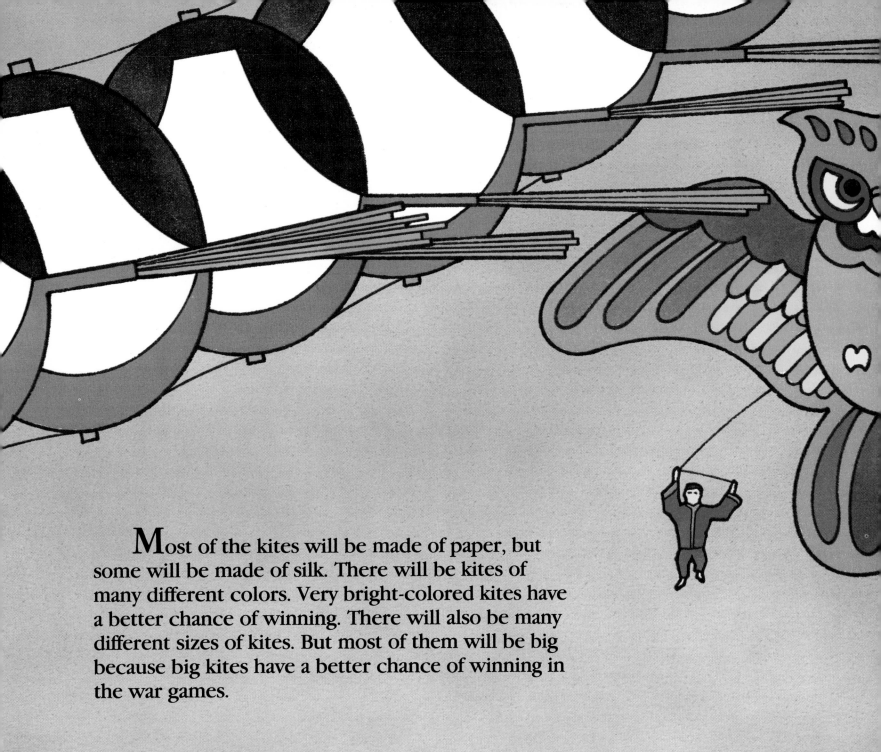

Most of the kites will be made of paper, but some will be made of silk. There will be kites of many different colors. Very bright-colored kites have a better chance of winning. There will also be many different sizes of kites. But most of them will be big because big kites have a better chance of winning in the war games.

Soon my mother and sister will have the food
ready, and then we will leave. It is a two-hour walk
from our house to the top of the mountain. We have
to walk through many streams, but it is worth
getting a little wet to go to the Chung Yang Chieh.
We walk with many other people, mostly my friends
and their families.

When we finally get to the top of the mountain, I take out my jade amulet and rub it between my hands. It is supposed to bring good luck.

The women will have the big feast ready by
the time the showing of the kites and the wars have
ended. Since nobody carries tables to the top of the
mountain, everyone brings tablecloths to put on the
ground. Everyone also brings delicious food. It will
take all day long to eat all the food.

All the boys and men get their kites ready. One of the ladies tells us to put our kites into the air. When they are all in the air, everybody begins doing stunts with their kites.

My kite looks beautiful in the air. It looks like a goldfish swimming. Everyone thinks mine is the best kite, so I win the kite showing contest. I am very happy.

Then comes the hardest part of all . . . the kite wars. It is going to be hard to cut some of the kite strings, but I have been practicing five hours a day for a long time. So I should have a good chance of winning.

One by one, I beat people. When we finally get down to the last five, it gets really hard. They are the winners from the last five years of the Chung Yang Chieh.

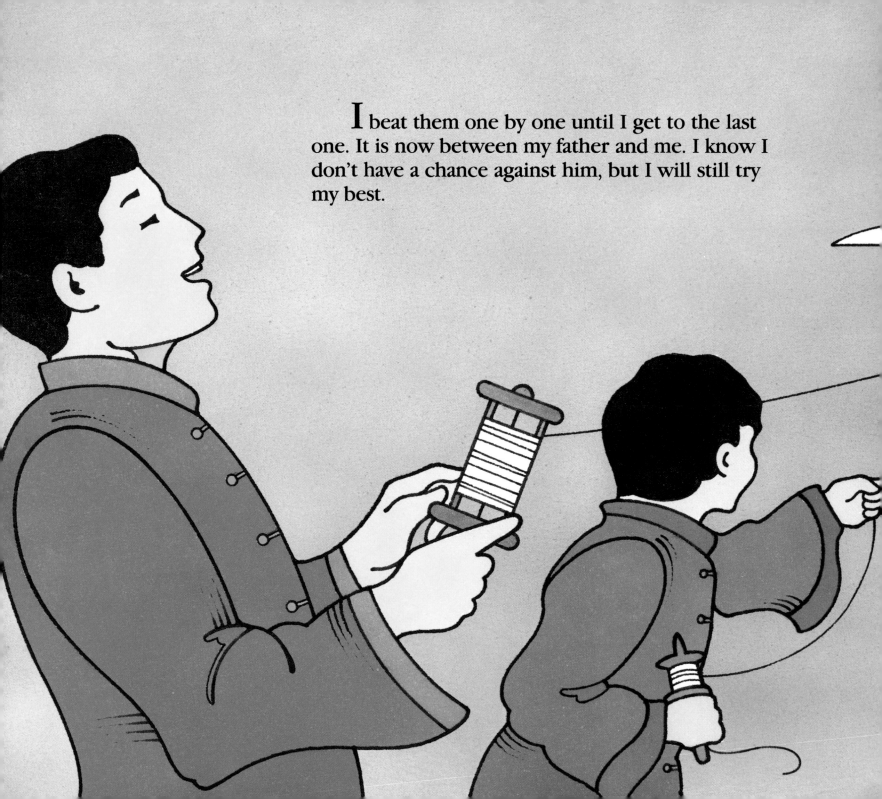

I beat them one by one until I get to the last one. It is now between my father and me. I know I don't have a chance against him, but I will still try my best.

He beat me. But to this day, even with my own grandson competing against me, I still think that was the best day of my life. Even the food tasted better then, it seems. And even though I have won many times since then, I will never forget that day.

Michael Reeser was born in Tacoma, Washington. When Michael was three and one-half years old, he and his older sister, Shawn, moved to Gilmer, Texas, to live with their grandparents. Michael and his family love animals. They have a dog, two cats, and a number of other animals.

Michael enjoys outdoor sports, camping, and fishing. He also enjoys constructing models, especially airplanes. He likes school a lot, especially because of the friends one can make there. Making friends is very important to Michael.

Michael thinks that he might become an electrical engineer some day. But he enjoys writing and thinks he might like to become a writer.

When he wrote his winning story, Michael was in sixth grade. His story was sponsored by his teacher, Barbara Campbell. Michael's story grew out of his fascination with China, which he explored through books from his county library. Chung Yang Chieh, the kite flying holiday in his book, was Michael's own invention.

The twenty honorable-mention winners in the **Raintree Publish-A-Book Contest** were: April Maria Burke, Old Town, Maine; Christine Debelak, Cleveland, Ohio; Aaron M. Eddy, Crossett, Arkansas; Tanisha Feacher, Homestead A.F.B., Florida; Brandon Geist, Schwenksville, Pennsylvania; Neal Kappenberg, North Bellmore, New York; Meegan Kelso, Coeur d'Alene, Idaho; Erin Mailath, Onalaska, Wisconsin; Olivia Julian Mendez, Richmond, California; Arnie Niekamp, Findlay, Ohio; Rebecca Papp, Hacienda Heights, California; Angela Rodrigues, San Lorenzo, California; Kirsten Ruckdeschel, Webster Groves, Missouri; Hannah Schneider, Washington, D.C.; Tres Sisson, Kaufman, Texas; Jenny Stalica, Buffalo, New York; Kenneth E. Stice, Des Arc, Arkansas; Kelley Tuggle, Largo, Florida; Regan Marie Valdes, Tampa, Florida; Scott Yoshikawa, San Jose, California.

Dick Sakahara grew up in Pasadena, California. He graduated from U.C.L.A. with a degree in design. He spends his vacations traveling and collecting folk art. Dick lives in Rancho Palos Verdes, California, with his wife, Arleen, a junior high school teacher.

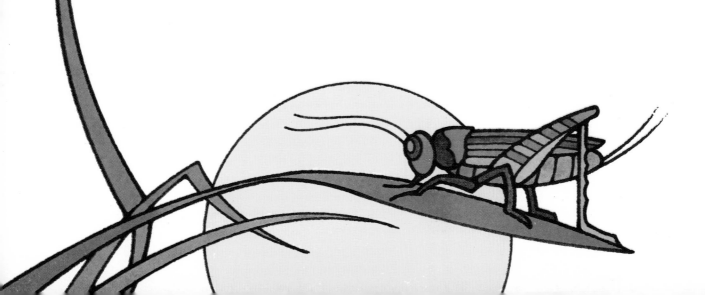